# BELIEVE IN SPRING

BELIEVE IN LOVE BOOK #8

## AMY SPARLING

CHAPTER ONE

Keanna

Awesome. My last mid-term of the semester is complete and I'm pretty sure I aced it. All that studying of historical facts with Jett last night helped solidify the information in my mind, and I was one of the first students in my massive class to finish taking the test. If only everything in life was as simple as memorizing a bunch of dates and definitions.

The warm spring sun welcomes me as I step out of the freezing cold college building. I swear, it's like they use ninety percent of our tuition money to keep the air conditioner running twenty four hours a day. But it's not my problem for the next nine days, because it's finally Spring Break.

I check my phone and find one new text from my adoptive mom, Becca.

*If you get out soon enough, come by La Tapitia for some lunch! I'm meeting Bay at 1.*

I check the time, and grin when I see I got out at the perfect time to meet them. Jumping in my Mustang that's all shiny and smells good since Jett washed it for me recently, I head toward the best Mexican restaurant in town.

It's a little busier than usual, but I guess Friday before Spring Break has everyone in a go-out-and-celebrate mood. I park across from my mom's car and head into the packed restaurant.

The hostess table at the front has at least two dozen people standing around waiting to be seated. I need to squeeze through them to go find my mom and her best friend inside, but I don't want to be rude, so I kind of stand here a minute. Eventually, the crowd thins as a hostess takes a large group to their table.

I slide up behind two women who smell like they donned a little too much perfume this morning, but they're blocking my way into the restaurant. I should just ask them to move over a bit, but being bold and standing up for myself has never been my strong suit.

"Da-aamn," one of the women says in this overly sexual way that catches my attention. "Don't make it obvious," she says, turning toward her friend, "but check out the guys behind me."

Her friend peeks over her shoulder, then her eyes widen and she grins. "Oh hell yes. We should ask if they want company," she says, primping her hair. "I want the one on the left. No—right. Hell, I don't care. I'll take them both."

Her friend pushes her playfully in the arm. "You have to leave one for me. I'll take either one, they're both hot as hell."

I wonder if they know they're being loud enough for me, a total stranger, to overhear every word. They shift over to get a better peek at the hot guys, and I find a way around them, only to see exactly who they're talking about.

My dad and Jett's dad.

I burst out laughing, unable to hold it back. Knowing the women are totally watching me right now, I walk quickly up to Park, the man who adopted me and pretty much saved my life, and say, "Hey guys! Have you seen that amazing artwork by the door?" I point to the door, which makes it look like I'm pointing to the women who are gawking at them.

Jace and Park look right at them, trying to find the artwork, and the women turn a deep shade of red and turn around.

I laugh. "Never mind, you can't really see it from here. So what are ya'll doing here?"

"My wife said they were getting some Mexican food, and we happened to be nearby so we decided we also wanted Mexican food," Jace explains. He pulls back the chair next to him. "Have a seat, kiddo."

I'm twenty years old, but he still calls me that.

"Where are they?" I ask, secretly hoping those two women will still be watching when the guys they were drooling over have beautiful wives join them at the table.

"Bathroom," my dad says.

A few seconds later, my mom and Bayleigh appear, but the drooling women are gone. Damn. We place our order with the waiter.

"How'd your test go?" Mom asks me.

"Really good," I say. "I think I'll be keeping my 4.0 intact."

She squeezes my hand. "I'm so proud of you."

My mom's hair is darker since she recently dyed it, and I think it makes her look younger than it did when she had it highlighted. I can notice the very fine wrinkles on the corners of her eyes, the ones she hates and always complains about, but they make me smile. Those wrinkles are there because she cares. She worries and she loves and she actually cares about me.

"Where are the babies?" I ask, feeling stupid that it's been like ten minutes and I didn't think about my own little brother. Jett also has a little sister and they are usually always with our moms.

"At the track," Mom says. "Betsy is watching them."

Jace says my name. "So are you excited for this week?"

"I'm excited about the time off school, and the races, but not the driving," I say with a laugh.

Jace nods. "There is too much driving in motocross. It's ridiculous."

"Jett makes it fun, but it's still hours of driving, so it can only get *so* fun before it's awful." I say, curling my lip.

He has three arenacross races this week and instead of being stuck at home in school, I'm going with him this time. The first race is in Dallas, then

San Antonio a few days later, and two days after that, we'll be driving to Vegas. You can't fly when you have to haul your own dirt bike. Team Loco, which is Jett's sponsorship team, doesn't have any official races this week, so Jett is racing arenacross both for fun, and to keep up his standing as the man to beat. Right now he's ranked number one in his racing class in the whole region. I can't wait until the nationals race where he'll become number one in the whole country.

"Remember that time we drove from Texas to California?" My dad says to my mom.

Her eyes widen. "Oh my god, that was the worst! I mean it ended up being fun, but the initial drive sucked. You had to get a new truck and everything."

"Wow," I say. "When did that happen?"

Mom smiles like she does when she's recalling something special. "Years ago. We were supposed to fly, and then the airport was closed, and then his truck broke down, so we had to buy a new one, and then all the hotels were booked—"

"It was Christmas," Dad says. He looks at my mom and his eyes soften. "But we made it special, right?"

She melts up against his shoulder. "Yes, we did."

I smile, even though it's a little awkward seeing them in one of their special romantic moments. My phone vibrates from my purse, and I bend down to get it.

"Hello?" I say.

"Heyyy babe," Jett says back. His voice always makes my knees week. Good thing I'm sitting. "How was your test?"

"It was good. How was your practice?"

"It was perfection, as always," he says with a chuckle. I can tell he's a little out of breath which means he just got done riding. He's probably covered in sweat, with the veins bulging on his muscles, which is literally the hottest state he can be in. It's a shame I'm not there to witness it.

"I'm eating lunch with the parents," I say.

"Which parents?"

"All of them."

He laughs. "You poor thing. Have they embarrassed the hell out of you yet?"

"Not yet, but once they realize who I'm talking to, I'm sure they will."

That gets Jace's attention and he turns to me. "Talking to Jett?" he asks.

"Nope," I say quickly. "I'm talking to a platonic girl friend."

"Is that why you're blushing?" Dad says.

"Oh my God, ya'll are the worst," I say.

On the phone, Jett laughs. "I'm sorry, baby. When you get done, come home. I need your help packing."

"Don't worry, " I say, giving the parents the evil eye as they playfully make fun of me for being so in love. "I'll be there soon."

CHAPTER TWO

Jett

Keanna sounded like she was in a great mood on the phone. It's nice to see the stress of the school year evaporate, if only for a little while. I'm so proud of her for doing this college thing. I'm not even in college yet, and honestly, I don't even want to go. Here's hoping the motocross gig earns me enough money to retire early. Keanna is the star in this relationship. She's the smart one, even if she doesn't think so. She's the one who takes care of me and makes my life so much easier.

I put up my bike and head inside to take a quick shower before she gets here. Tomorrow we'll be heading to Dallas bright and early in the morning, so she's coming to spend the night with me tonight. Sometimes I wish she'd just stay over here every single night, but since we're neighbors, it's not that hard to see each other. Keanna says it would be too weird if she stayed every night, because it'd be like she was living with me while I live with my parents. I totally get where she's coming from, even though my parents are pretty damn cool.

As I shower, I think back to the life I had before I met her. I was going down a shitty path in life, much the same as most of the guys I know in motocross. Dating whoever, whenever, hooking up with hot girls just for the fun of it. I know my dad hated it, and I can't blame him. When I met Keanna, I fell hard for the girl. All that other shit in my past just disappeared in an instant, and now, even thinking about the idea of random hookups makes me feel sick to my stomach. How could a guy want to live a life like that when you can have a perfect girlfriend every single day?

I love my parents, but I think it's a little more than obvious that they love Keanna more than me now. I snort out a laugh as I get out of the shower and get dressed. Keanna is the girl who saved me from a reckless and stupid path in life. They have every reason to love her, and I'm glad they do.

After I get dressed, I stare at the open suitcase on my bed. It's huge enough for Keanna to crawl inside and zip up—we know because we tried it out for fun once—and it's black with the blue Team Loco logo on it. I could bring anything I want to, and yet I suck at packing. Right now I have three pairs of jeans, some sleep shorts, a few boxers, and some socks.

I freaking hate packing. I always forget something, from my phone charger to a knee brace or that one time when I forgot to bring my toothbrush but brought two tubes of toothpaste instead. Packing is the worst.

"I'm here," Keanna calls out, her voice faint as it travels from downstairs all the way up to my room.

"In my room," I call back. "I need help!"

I can hear her angelic laugh as she jogs up the stairs. "Let me guess?" she says, appearing in my doorway. "Your suitcase is too vast and big and you have no idea what to put in it?"

"Yep," I say, meeting her at the door. I slide my

arms around her waist and pull her close. She smells like green apple shampoo and a little like a Mexican restaurant.

"You're a grown man, you know that right?" she says playfully, her nails scratching lightly down my back as I hold her close to me. "Nineteen years old and you can't even pack a suitcase."

"I can pack it, I'm just not good at it." I make a pouty face and she rolls her eyes.

"Don't worry, I got you."

I slide my hands under her ass and lift her off the floor. She wraps her legs around my waist as I carry her to my bed and sit her down carefully. "I love you," I whisper, my lips against hers.

"Do you love me, or do you love my packing skills?" she whispers back.

I kiss her. "Both."

She laughs and pushes me away. "Let's see what train wreck you've assembled here," she says, going through my clothing. "There's not a single shirt… were you planning on spending all week showing off those abs?"

I lift my shirt and flex the six pack I work so hard to maintain. "Sounds like a plan to me."

She rolls her eyes and stands up, heading to my closet. "I will get you some shirts, you dork."

I turn on my TV and set it to the YouTube app so we can listen to music. "Are you packed yet?"

"Yeah, I left my suitcase downstairs by the back door because it's ridiculously heavy," Keanna says. "I brought those books for Aiden's sister."

"She'll love that," I say. Aiden is also on Team Loco, and he has a little sister who is as obsessed with reading as Keanna is. She had an extra set of some teen romance series after she won an autographed set online, so she promised to give it to her.

I walk up behind Keanna while she takes my clothes off hangers and folds them neatly into my suitcase. I slide my hands up her back and rub her shoulders. I hear her release a soft sigh, see her head tilt to the side as I massage her back. But she keeps working, diligently sorting my outfits for the week. I lean forward and kiss her neck. She freezes.

"Baby, I can't focus if you do that."

"Who needs focus?" I whisper, kissing her again. I grab her waist and tug her up against me.

She giggles. "Let me finish packing and then we can continue this."

I heave a big sarcastic sigh and then rest my chin on her shoulder, watching her continue to fold clothes and ignore me hanging out behind her. "Okay, I guess I can wait."

"Such a horn dog," she mutters, but I can hear the smile in her voice.

"I upgraded to the paid Spotify subscription so we'll have awesome tunes while we drive," I say, trying to change the subject since I'm all ready to strip her clothes off and throw her on the bed. "Should make the trip more fun."

"Awesome," she says. "I've been to Dallas and San Antonio a million times, but I'm excited for Vegas."

"Yeah?" I say, watching her face light up with excitement.

She nods. "It sucks that we aren't old enough to drink, but I can't wait to see the Strip all lit up at night. And I want to try that Vegas Cupcakes place. All their cupcakes are ridiculously fancy and are supposed to be the best ones in the country. I think it'll be awesome. It'll be even better if you win your race."

I grin and watch her work, helping me once again do something I'm not good at. This girl is my angel. Vegas will be really fun because we'll have three days there and I only race one of those days.

Maybe I'll find a place in Vegas that would make the perfect spot…

I grin as my heart fills with anticipation and excitement.

Yes. Vegas.

Maybe I'll do it then.

# CHAPTER THREE

Keanna

Jett is being a lot more affectionate than usual. I mean, it's not like he's ever been distant or cold toward me, but lately it's like he's metal and I'm magnetized and he can't stay away from me. I like it, but it makes me wonder. Is he being overly affectionate to make up for something I don't know about?

I try to shrug the thoughts away. I remind myself that Jett is mine, and he's the greatest guy ever, and he's loyal and loving and would never lie to me. It helps a little.

I check the time on my phone—it's three in the morning. I keep falling asleep and then waking up half an hour later, filled with bad thoughts about Jett and worries over nothing. I roll over and look at Jett in the darkness. The moonlight filters in through the window just a little, and I can make out the outline of his face sleeping peacefully next to me. I scoot a little closer and rest my head on his shoulder.

On instinct, his arm goes around me. His breath stays steady, and he remains asleep, but even when totally passed out, he remembers to hold onto me. It warms my heart and I slip back to sleep, telling myself I was stupid to worry about anything.

WE ARRIVE IN DALLAS, TEXAS AROUND TEN IN THE morning. There's a stadium next door to the hotel we're staying at and that's where the arenacross races will be tomorrow. For now, we have the day to rest and Jett plans on taking it easy to prepare for the race tomorrow.

"This hotel is pretty nice," Jett says as we step off the elevators on the tenth floor.

"Damn," a voice calls out from down the hallway. I recognize it immediately as Zach Pena, a fellow Team Loco racer. "They let anyone in here!" he says, winking at me. "I thought this hotel was for classy people only," he says to Jett.

"You should have known it wasn't the second they let your country ass in here," Jett says, walking up and fist bumping his teammate. We may live in Texas, which is home of the cowboys, but Zach is from a small town in Tennessee and his southern twang puts Texans to shame.

After leaving our stuff in our hotel room, we meet up with Zach and the other two guys on Team Loco, Clay and Aiden. I usually feel like the odd one out when I'm with the guys, but it's been long enough now that I feel included. They don't rag on Jett for bringing his girlfriend, and they're all very nice to me so it works. Still, I think it'd be better if one of the other guys got a girlfriend so I'd have someone to hang out with while they do their thing. I don't really see that happening, though. Zach is a player who hooks up more than he dates girls, Clay only cares about dirt bikes so it's like women aren't even on his radar, and Zach cares more about earning money to help his family back home than meeting girls. But maybe one day it'll happen.

We head over to the stadium next door so the guys can get checked in for tomorrow's races. Since I'm Jett's VIP guest, I get a blue wristband that lets me into the races for free, and it also lets me into the special areas that spectators can't get into, like the starting line and the pits. I'm feeling a little more than special as I wrap the bracelet around my wrist.

I love the smell of arenacross tracks. It's a little weird, probably, but the exhaust mixed with fresh dirt has started to remind me of home. Dirt bikes are Jett's thing, and he is my home. The Track, the business my parents and Jett's parents own, is also home and that place is 99% dirt. So maybe it's not the smell of dirt that I'm attracted to, but the feelings that come with it. For the first time in my life I have a home. I am wanted, and I am loved.

I couldn't say so much about the first seventeen years of my existence. I was raised by a selfish woman who could never hold down a job or keep an apartment. Her relationships were crap and her idea of love was trying to get me to sleep with some creeper old guy in exchange for money.

Those days of my life seem so long ago now that I've moved on and joined another, much better family. I used to have nightmares about it, about her. But now my life is happy and my dreams are mostly good.

The guys get into the empty arena and one of the employees lets us walk the track. It's not the same as riding it, but seeing the layout lets the guys get a good vibe for how it'll be to race on it tomorrow.

I hold Jett's hand while we walk around on the dirt, and I stay mostly quiet while he and the guys talk nonstop. It's all dirt bike talk, which is mostly lost on me.

Eventually, we leave and walk back to our hotel, which only half a block away. The parking lot is filled with other racers and people who will set up vendor booths at the races tomorrow. Jett and the other guys say hello to a ton of people as we walk past them. I notice a few girls watching me, their eyes trailing from my face to my hand, which is still clasped in Jett's. I try not to let it make me feel awkward. After all, I'd be jealous if I were in their shoes. Everyone loves Jett Adams, but he only loves me.

Since it's nearly dinner time, the guys want to try out this steakhouse that's right across the road. Once we're there, I excuse myself to go pee and wash my hands. The restaurant is huge, so once I walk out of the bathroom, I can't remember which way I took to get here.

I stand near a large potted plant and casually look around the tables, hoping to spot Jett before too long so I don't look like an idiot.

"That is definitely Jett," I hear someone say.

I look to my right and see two girls, about my age, sitting at the bar. They're turned around and staring toward the left. I follow their gaze and see my boyfriend sitting with Clay, Zach, and Aiden, and let out a sigh of relief. Two of Jett's fans saved me from getting lost. Go figure.

"...so fucking hot," I hear one of the girls say.

"They're all hot," the other one says back.

Curiosity takes over and I stay here behind this tree a little longer, just to hear what they're saying.

"Yeah, but Jett is hotter. He looks just like his dad."

"You should go talk to him instead of sitting here lusting after him," her friend says.

The girl wiggles her eyebrows. "Maybe I will …

I don't see that slut girlfriend of his. Looks like he's free for the taking."

A knot of anger twists in my stomach. Just because Jett has a girlfriend doesn't mean she's a slut. It doesn't mean I'm a slut. Why are girls so freaking mean to each other?

"Ugh, I forgot about that hoe," the friend says, curling her lip in disgust. "Are they still a thing? They can't possibly still be together. She looks like backwoods trailer trash."

"Last time I checked, they were," the first girl says.

Hot tears threaten to spill from my eyes, but I blink them away. Maybe it's because her comment hit too close to home, but I'm totally pissed off right now. I was born and raised as white trash. So what? That's not who I am anymore. And Jett shouldn't be insulted for who he's dating.

I step away from the potted plant and walk right up them. Their eyes widen when they see me, and I make a big deal of looking at what the first girl is wearing. A low-cut tank top and short shorts with fishnet stockings underneath them. Her makeup looks like a kid put it on, trying their hardest to be sexy.

"Take a look at the two of us," I say, standing

tall and holding my head high. "Which one of us seems more like a slut? Because it's not me."

Her mouth hangs open like the idiot she is, and with a satisfied smile, I turn and walk toward my boyfriend.

CHAPTER FOUR

Jett

can feel the adrenaline coursing through my veins. The races start in half an hour, and I'm pumped, mentally and physically. I've officially been racing dirt bikes for most of my life and yet the adrenaline never goes away. It's always there, ready to take over the moment the gate drops and I speed off, competing with twenty four other racers for that coveted first place trophy.

Lucky for me, arenacross is a little easier than professional supercross. Not technically, since the track is still a beast to navigate, but the rest of the racers are a step below me in talent. Only a few of them have large sponsorships like me and the guys from Team Loco, so I have a feeling the top three places will be dominated by our blue and black jerseys. We'll make our manager proud.

Keanna watches me get ready. I gave her my VIP pass so she's allowed down here in the pits with me while all the other spectators have to stay up in the stadium seats. I buckle up my boots, throw on my jersey, fasten my neck brace, and then look around for my helmet.

"Right here," she says, holding out my helmet.

"Thank you babe." I take it and lean over and kiss her.

"Not fair," Clay calls out from a few feet over where he's also getting dressed. "It's one thing to bring your girlfriend here, but another to rub it in our faces how happy you are."

"Dude, no one's stopping you from getting your own girlfriend."

He snorts as he pulls the Velcro tight on his gloves. "Eyes on the prize, Adams. I don't have time for girls when I'm too busy trying to beat you."

Keanna watches him with this curious look on

her face, and if I didn't know any better, I'd think she's trying to think of someone to set him up with. I know it bothers her that she's the only girl-friend on the team and often feels left out when I bring her to places like this.

I slip on my helmet and poke her in the side. She's wearing black workout leggings and a blue Team Logo T-shirt and she looks so damn sexy in those tight ass pants. I feel like a pig and a caveman when she's all sexy like that because I know it makes all the other guys jealous, and I don't care. I love it, actually. I've got the hot girl and they've got nothing but jealousy.

I poke her ribs again and she squirms. "That tickles."

"Meet me at the finish line?"

She smiles. "You better be the first one across it."

Aiden jogs up and smacks the back of my helmet. "Ready? I'm about to line up."

"Sounds good," I say. I crank up my bike and let it idle for a minute, and then I turn back to my beautiful girlfriend.

"Twenty laps," I say, taking her face in my hands.

"So longggg," she says with a groan.

"It'll be over before you know it."

"And then boring San Antonio, and then onto awesome Vegas!" Her smile reaches her eyes when she mentions Vegas, and once again I'm feeling like that'll be the perfect time to do it.

"Only a few days away," I say.

She reaches up and kisses the front of my helmet. "Good luck."

"Love you," I say.

"Love you more," she says back.

Keanna waits with the other VIPs, who are mostly older mechanics, managers, and parents, and waves to me as I set up my bike on the starting line. The starting line is a long stretch, and you draw a number to see which spot you'll get. I drew a shitty number so I'm right smack in the middle of the line instead of on the edge like I'd prefer. In the middle, you have to make sure to be the fastest at the drop or you'll get stuck behind other people, and possibly end up in a pile up of bikes at the first turn. Not that I can't pull away from something like that and regain first place during the twenty laps, but it's a lot more annoying.

Soon the air fills with the roar of two dozen dirt bikes, and I steady my attention to the starting gate. It drops, and I pin the throttle, my focus solely on the race now.

With luck and talent, I manage to get the holeshot so I'm out in front of everyone. Now I just need to keep it for the next twenty laps.

Which is exactly what I do. I'm not trying to be some egotistical prick, but when Keanna is here watching me, I have way more drive to race hard and fast. Sometimes when I'm traveling with Team Loco, I can feel myself getting lazy after the tenth lap, but this time I don't stop. I ride hard and I keep the throttle pinned, and before long the checkered flag whips out, signaling that I've won the race. I turn the bike sideways as I soar over the finish line jump, and then my heart beats faster knowing that I'm about to see her again. It's so much more fun having my girl with me at these things. I can't wait until this semester is over and she can spend the rest of summer with me traveling and racing. Hopefully she wants that, too.

Sweat pours off me as I slow down and ride to my slot in the pits, which is right between the other Team Loco guys. Clay is right on my tail, so he was probably second place. I see Aiden and Zach a few seconds later. I park my bike on the stand and rip off my helmet, then grab a bottle of water from a nearby ice chest. I glance around and see her walking quickly toward me.

"You were amazing," she says, her eyes sparkling under the bright stadium lights. "I always love watching you race."

I bend down and kiss her lightly so that my sweat-drenched body doesn't touch her.

Zach comes by and shakes my hand. "Dude, good race."

"Thanks, man."

"Showers and then dinner?" Aiden says as he rubs a towel over his sweating head. "Shower separately, and then eat together, is what I meant just in case you pervs thought otherwise."

Clay snorts. "I'm down. I'm starving."

Keanna shifts on her feet and even though she's smiling, I get the feeling she feels a little out of place with the guys.

"I think we're gonna head back to the hotel," I say, giving her a quick wink when she looks up at me. "You guys go on."

"Look at him," Aiden says sarcastically. "Always rubbing it in with the girlfriend."

I flip him off and he laughs. "See ya'll in San A?"

"Yeah, man. See you tomorrow."

After packing up my bike and all my gear, we

head back to the hotel. I head straight to the bath-room to rip off my sweaty riding gear, and Keanna calls my name.

"What's up?" I call back.

"Your phone is ringing. It's Zach."

"Let it ring," I call back.

When I get out of the shower, Keanna is sitting on the hotel's desk chair, her face tight with worry.

"What is it?"

"Your phone has been ringing like nonstop. All of the guys have called you like twice each, and I wanted to answer it because I thought maybe it's an emergency but I didn't want to go through your stuff..."

"Babe," I say, holding the towel around my waist as I lean over and kiss her. "My stuff is your stuff. I hope the guys are okay."

I grab my phone off the nightstand and unlock the screen. I have a dozen missed calls and a few text messages.

"What is it?" Keanna asks.

I click on the first message. Shit.

"Well?" Keanna says, her voice growing impatient.

"Uh..." I don't know what to say. I am

temporarily out of words. I turn off my phone and toss it on the bed. "It's um, nothing."

"Doesn't seem like nothing," she says, standing up. "Why do you look like that?"

I bite my lip. "It's … well, it's about you."

CHAPTER FIVE

Keanna

"*Don't worry, none of us believe any of that shit,*" Jett says, as he reads a text from one of the guys. Their words mean nothing to me. I am already worried and I haven't seen what's going on yet.

"Would you please tell me what the hell is going on?"

Jett turns to me, his eyes slowly meeting mine. "It's nothing, babe. Someone just decided to talk trash about you online."

I groan. "What is it this time?"

"It's nothing."

I hold out my hand. "I want to see it."

With a pained frown, Jett hands me his phone. Someone has sent him a link to a Twitter post. I click it, and the Twitter app opens to a very long thread. I see my name, and my heart pounds as I scroll up to the start of the long post that's bashing me.

And then I start reading, and my entire life flashes before my eyes. Not the good life I have now, with family and a little brother and a great boyfriend. My old life. The life that almost broke me.

We were in Phoenix. My biological mom, Dawn, and me. It was the longest we'd lived in one place in a long time, and I was starting to feel settled down in my school. It was freshman year. I had a couple of friends who would sit with me at lunch. One day they invited me over for a party, and I was eager to go. I'd worn my best jeans and shirt, which wasn't saying much, and stole some of my mom's makeup in an attempt to look prettier. Then I walked the fifteen blocks to the girl's house. I remember her name was Mindy, and she was really popular despite living in a run-down trailer. Where I came from, all the popular people were rich, but not in this case. Mindy was pretty and outgoing and a lot of fun. Later, I'd realize that her popularity stemmed from the fact that she'd sleep with any guy who wanted it, but at the time I had no idea. I was just happy to be included. I was out at a party with lots of people, drinking free beer, and trying to enjoy myself, and it was a lot better than sitting at home where we didn't have a TV or internet or anything fun.

Mindy bumped into me with her shoulder. "I see you staring at him," she'd said, making flirty eyes at me.

I probably turned beet red as I shook my head and said I wasn't staring at anyone. But she knew I was lying. "His name is JJ," she said, nudging me with her cup of beer. "Go say hi."

I did. I don't know why, but I did.

JJ was tall, older, and cute in this rugged bad boy way. I'd only been watching him because he was sitting alone on a couch and looked just as bored as I was. But with Mindy's encouragement, I walked right up to him and sat down on the other side of the couch.

"Hello," I said meekly when he looked at me.

"Yo," he said back.

And that was that, for about ten minutes. Then

Mindy sauntered over and sat herself between us, throwing an arm around both of our shoulders. "JJ, this is Keanna. She has a crush on you," she'd said entirely too loudly. I wanted to drop dead of mortification, but JJ just looked at me like he'd suddenly seen me in a new light. "Cool," he said with a nod and a sly grin in my direction.

"My work here is done," Mindy said, just before hopping up and disappearing into the crowd.

"So how do you know Mindy?" JJ asked me.

"We go to school together," I said.

He slid a little closer and kept up the conversation. We talked for a few minutes about nothing in particular, and my heart was pounding a mile a minute.

"You want to find somewhere more quiet to talk?" he said.

And I remember it very clearly because he said *to talk*. Not anything else. Talk. I was a total idiot back then and assumed that what he said was what he'd meant. I said yes. He stood up and took my hand and I was so excited that I guy was holding my hand that I let him lead me down the hallway and into a tiny bedroom at the end of the house. He closed the door behind us and then twisted the lock, securing us from the outside world. My stomach flipped.

Then his arms were all over me, pawing at me like some rabid beast. His tongue was hot and tasted gross as it shoved in my mouth. I froze for a second, not knowing what to do. I'll admit, part of me kind of wanted to make out a little, just to know what it was like. He was cute, after all, and he clearly liked me. But then he got too handsy, and he reeked of alcohol, and I panicked.

"I want to take things slow!" I said, my words rushed and panicked and stupidly shaking from my fear.

He jumped back as if I'd electrocuted him. Then he chuckled and ran a hand through his hair. "Baby girl, I don't take things slow. I think you got the wrong idea here."

"What do you mean?" I stuttered out.

He laughed, a cruel sound that made me feel very small. "I don't want to date you. You're Mindy's friend, which means you're just good for a hookup."

Those words stayed with me for months. Even after Dawn uprooted us again and we moved to another town, I still thought about it all the time. I wasn't the kind of girl worthy of a relationship. I was just a hookup. A loser. Not girlfriend material.

But that wasn't the worst part. Just two weeks after the party, I'd come home from school to find my mom hooking up with a guy on the couch.

"Dammit!" she cursed when I walked into the room. "You're not supposed to be home yet!"

I just ran into my bedroom and closed the door to give her privacy with her guest, and didn't bother telling her that this was the exact time I got home from school every day. I'd only seen them for a fraction of a second, but it was all I needed.

My mom was hooking up with JJ. And he saw me too.

Shame falls over me as I scroll through these tweets, disregarding Jett's plea for me to just ignore it.

Some girl is tweeting the whole story, but she's embellishing it a lot.

*Let me tell you something about Jett Adam's girlfriend,* she begins in the first tweet. *I happened to meet one of her old boyfriends, and he had something to say about her. Not only is she a big slut, her mother is, too.*

It only gets worse from there. The tweets say that I had been sleeping with JJ, and all of his friends, for weeks. And that my mom also slept with them. I'm called every bad name in the book, and then my reputation is dragged as far down as it can go.

*She was begging for any guy to sleep with her*, the tweets continue. *And after I asked around online, I got many people to confirm this.*

"This is all a lie," I tell Jett, tears filling my eyes. "You know this is a lie, right? I never slept with anyone!"

Jett's lips are pressed into a frown. "I know, baby. No one believes that shit. It's probably just some fan who is obsessed with me. Please don't read any more of it."

Tears pour down my cheeks. I click on the tiny picture of the person who posted all these tweets and look at her profile. Her name is Tawny, and she lives in Dallas. I zoom in on her picture, and realize that this is all my fault. It's the girl from the steakhouse. The one I called a slut.

Looks like I didn't have the final word, after all.

CHAPTER SIX

Jett

I am full of rage, and wish I could hit something. But you can't hit the Internet, which is filled with anonymous assholes. Whoever this bitch is that started a tirade against my girlfriend is going to pay for it. But first, I have to take care of my girl.

"Baby, no one will care about this shit," I say, wrapping her in my arms and resting my head on top of hers. I can tell she's trying hard to hold back tears, but it's not working. "Seriously."

"It already has a ton of likes," she says, her voice

muffled as I hold her close. "People do care. They're already saying you deserve better than me."

I cringe. I was hoping she didn't see that part on Twitter. Someone announced that I should break up with her, and lots of people retweeted it and agreed. I don't understand what makes the fans think they can get involved with my personal life. Those aren't the type of people I want rooting for me on the track. Those people can take their drama elsewhere.

I rub my hand down Keanna's back. "Let's do something to take your mind off this," I say softly.

She pulls away. "I think I'm going to go shower."

"Want me to come with you?" I ask, giving her a flirty look.

She steps back and shakes her head. "I just want to be alone. Just … please … just leave me alone for a while."

It kills me to see her like this, but I know that she's serious when she asks for time by herself.

"Okay," I say. "Take your time."

She grabs some clothes from her suitcase and slips into our hotel's bathroom. I hear the water turn on, and I sit here feeling so damn hopeless.

On my phone, I report the girl who posted all those horrible things about Keanna, and then I block her. I scroll down and find every person who was saying anything remotely rude about my girlfriend and I block them, too.

Then I think carefully about my wording and I post a tweet to my profile.

*Anyone who spreads untrue rumors, or says hateful things about me, my girlfriend, or anyone I care about is not a fan of mine. Don't come to my races. Don't buy my merch. Kindly fuck off.*

I feel a little better after posting the tweet, and the replies and likes start coming in quickly, so I close the app to make sure I don't get caught up in the stupid online drama. People can be so cruel. I don't understand what goes through some of these girl's heads. Do they think that calling my girlfriend a slut will make me dump her and then ask them out? Never happening.

Even if Keanna and I didn't last forever, I'd never date a rude fan. You can't trust them because they're in it for the fame. I grind my teeth and stand up, needing to get all of this anger out of my system. I don't even like thinking about it. Keanna and I are never splitting up. Not if I have anything to do with it.

I decide to step outside and take a walk down the hotel's long empty corridor. It doesn't help clear my mind any, so I call my dad. He always knows what to do.

"Hey, Dad," I say when he answers.

"What's wrong? I saw you got first place so you shouldn't sound so upset, son."

I take a deep breath. "I already forgot about the race actually," I say.

"Why's that?" Dad is always there for me. Because he's younger than my friend's dads, maybe he understands better. Or maybe he's just a better person in general. Whatever it is, I'm never embarrassed to talk to him about what's going on.

"Have you seen the drama online?"

He snorts. "I rarely ever go online."

My dad's not big into social media, so I guess that makes sense. At least this drama hasn't spread very far yet. Maybe it will just stay on Twitter.

I sigh. "Some bitch got on Twitter and spread a bunch of horrible lies about Keanna. Calling her a slut and stuff. And then other fangirls piled on and they're all attacking her online."

"Damn, people are the worst," Dad says. "How's Keanna?"

"Not good. She wanted to be left alone, so I'm walking the hallways of the hotel."

"You should go to her," Dad says.

I shake my head. "It doesn't work like that. If she wants to be alone, I have to respect that. I just feel so shitty. She's not being attacked for who she is, but for who she's dating. It's all my fault that these girls are targeting her. I hate it."

"I know the feeling," he says after a moment. "You can't let it get to you. Stick by your girl and ignore everything else."

"That's what I'm trying to do."

"That's what you will do," he says. "You've got this, son. Just be strong for her and she'll know you've got her back. She's probably not mad about what the people were saying, but about how you'll react to it."

"I'm not going to leave her," I say quickly.

Dad laughs. "I know. But trust me, that's how girls are. They'll worry that you *will* leave. That's how your mom was. It never hurts to remind them that you're not going anywhere."

"Okay," I say, reaching the end of the hallway. I turn around and walk back toward my hotel room. "I'll do that."

"You're heading to San Antonio tomorrow?" Dad asks.

"Yeah, leaving at six in the morning."

"Drive safe. Your sister misses you."

I snort. "That's because I'm the only one who knows how to play a decent game of peek-a-boo."

"That might be true," Dad says with a laugh. "Good luck tomorrow, Jett."

"Thanks, Dad."

"And don't worry," he says. "This will blow over."

I hope so. I really hope it does. Because I never want to see Keanna looking that upset again.

CHAPTER SEVEN

Keanna

The drive to San Antonio is silent. Jett plays some music softly on the radio but I know neither one of us listens to it. I don't want to talk. I don't know what to say. I thought about trying to fake like everything is normal and A-Okay and fine and put on a cheery smile and deal with this, but Jett knows me better than that. He'd see right through the fake happiness, and that would be worse than just being myself. Right now, myself doesn't want to talk, so I don't. I sit here and stare out the window for the whole drive.

Once we arrive at our new hotel which is also next to the stadium for the races tomorrow, Jett reaches over and squeezes my hand. "I love you," he says.

"I love you too," I say back. It's not a lie, and he knows it.

We take our stuff into the hotel and check in. Our room is on the first floor, which kind of sucks because I like looking out windows of somewhere high up so I can see the whole town below.

Not two seconds after we make it into our hotel room does someone knock on the door. Loudly. Annoyingly.

"Open up!" Clay yells. "We've been here for hours!"

Jett opens the door and the three guys from his team all barrel into our room. "It's been more like half an hour," Aiden says. "But we didn't want to walk the track until you got here."

"Although I think we should get a sneak peek so we have a chance to beat you," Zach says to Jett, then he tosses a wink to me. "Not that it would help."

Jett laughs. "You want to go check out the track now?"

"Yeah, then we need dinner," Zach says.

Jett walks over to me and takes my hands in his. He lowers his voice so only I can hear. "Do you want me to tell them to go on without us?"

I stare into his eyes, feeling guilty for all the concern in them. He knows I'm hurting and he'll do whatever it takes to make me feel better. But this is his race, and we're here for him to advance his career. I can't just let it all go to hell because I feel like shit. I shake my head. "I think I'll stay here, but you go ahead."

He gives me a look like he really doesn't like that idea.

I put my hand on his chest. "Babe, I'm serious," I say with a little smile. "Go check out the track. I'm tired, and I just want to watch TV."

"Okay," he says, pulling me in to kiss my forehead. "Call me if you need anything."

I wave to the guys and as soon as they're gone, the door closed behind them, I rush up and twist the deadbolt into place. And then I rest my head against the cool wooden door and start to cry.

I know I should stay away and take Jett's advice and just ignore all the drama online, but I can't. I am weak, and pathetic. I am just as worthless as they say I am.

I sit on the edge of the crisply made hotel bed

and open up Twitter on my phone. It's bad enough that this girl blasted me online with lies and horrible name-calling, but she's even tagged me in some of them. My tears come harder as I scroll through the vile on Twitter.

There are a few people replying, telling me not to worry about those bitches, but their kind words don't help at all. The mean words cut into me, lashing my heart wide open. The few nice things here and there are nothing more than tiny bandages that don't help.

Jett's last tweet makes me smile a little. He's being an amazing boyfriend by standing up for me, which is more than I could have asked for. All of the replies to his post are nice, and I'm wondering if that's because he's blocked anyone who says anything negative. Probably. For the millionth time, I wish I had just kept my mouth shut at that restaurant. I should have let her talk about me to her friend. I should have walked away. But instead, I thought I was standing up for myself and all I did was make this girl dig up dirt on me and unleash it into the world. I'm used to being called a skank, or unworthy of Jett. That's been happening since the day we started dating. And it sucks and it hurts, but for the most part, I'm used to it.

This time it hurts worse. She brought up a person from my past. I've spent the last two years becoming a new person with a new life. I threw away all of the memories of my past the day my biological mother disowned me, and I've looked forward to a new life that's better.

But this just makes me realize something I hadn't thought of before. I can get a new last name and new parents and a new house, but I'll never stop being the girl I used to be. I was born trash and I'll always be trash. I tried to run away from it, but that didn't matter.

Jett will see through this one day, I know he will.

I drop my phone and bury my face into the pillow, letting the tears pour out for what feels like a very long time. Every time I close my eyes, I see that last tweet I read before turning off my phone.

That girl's words are burned into my memory, staring me right in the face.

*Jett deserves so much better than some trailer trash whore. We should make it our mission to convince him to leave her.*

I can't say I blame them. Yeah, I never actually slept with JJ, but my mom did. I was trash. I *am* trash. I still sit at a fancy restaurant with my family and wonder how they do this knife and fork thing with their food when I've never been taught how to eat all classy like that. I barely know anything about motocross. Jett deserves someone better. He deserves a girl that grew up in the sport and knows all about it. Maybe even a girl that also rides dirt bikes so they can go riding together.

Guilt weighs me down as I sit up and try to dry my tears. I know what they're saying on Twitter is true. Jett deserves better. But I still don't want to give him up. He is the best part of me.

There's a soft knock on the hotel door, and it makes me jump. "Delivery," someone calls out. It doesn't sound like any of the guys' voices, so I hope they're not playing a prank on me.

I wipe at my eyes and try to compose myself and then I open the door just a crack. A huge display of flowers fills the air. I open the door all the way and see a man from the hotel holding the huge bouquet.

"I have a delivery for you, ma'am," he says, handing over the flowers.

"Thank you," I say.

He grins and then turns away before I start crying again. I close the door and set the heavy vase down on a nearby table. Flowers of all colors burst out of the vase. Pinks and reds and purples and even sunflowers. It's absolutely beautiful and I can't believe Jett would do something so sweet. We'll be driving to Vegas in two days, so what am I supposed to do with these?

I take the little card off the flowers and open it up, surprised when I don't see Jett's handwriting on the card. I momentarily panic, thinking these flowers were meant for someone else, but then I read the message.

*Cheer up, Sweetheart. The people who matter love you, and the ones who don't can go to hell.*

*Love,*

*Clay, Zach, & Aiden*

More tears roll down my cheeks, but they are of the happy variety. I can't believe I'm smiling after spending the last hour feeling the worst I've ever felt. Having the approval of Jett's teammates makes me feel a whole lot better. Maybe they'll talk to him and encourage him not to leave me like the people on Twitter are asking him to do.

I lean in and smell the flowers and feel my heart start to repair itself. The world may be cruel, but there are still good people out there. And it sure as hell feels good to have someone on my side.

CHAPTER EIGHT

Jett

This isn't the first time I've lost a race. It's just like the unstoppable adrenaline I get before the gate drops—losing makes me feel like shit. I'll never get over it. I'll never lose a race and be like, meh, oh well. It always sucks.

This time my shitty third place finish wasn't due to me competing with faster racers than myself. They didn't have better agility or speed, or even bikes that were faster. In fact, their bikes are exactly the same because first and second place went to two of my teammates. That's a good thing

—Team Loco on the podium—but it still sucks for me.

The reason I lost is because I can't stop worrying about Keanna and the stupid drama that comes with being even mildly famous in a professional sport. It's not like I'm Ryan freaking Reynolds or anything. I'm just a guy who races in a sport most people don't even care about. I can't even imagine the bullshit real celebrities go through. I let the trolls online get in my head. I let it bother me, agitate me, and screw up my racing tonight.

I love Keanna with all my heart, but I tell her a teensy lie when I get back to the hotel after the San Antonio race. I squeeze my wrist and say it's been hurting. An old injury must be acting up again, and that's what made me ride so shitty. I think she believes it.

The guys sent her flowers, which I didn't know about beforehand, and that seems to have cheered her up. I wish I had thought of it, but I'm glad someone did. I know she likes being included in my life, and there's no better way than for Team Loco to show their support of her. I love those idiots. They're really good guys.

Keanna barely says a word while we eat dinner with the guys at a local Mexican restaurant. Then when we turn in for the night, she falls asleep quickly and doesn't wake up. I know, because I can't seem to stay asleep. I keep waking up and looking over at her, wanting to make sure she's okay. I wish she'd let me talk about it. But I guess talking won't help much. The sad fact is that jealous girls online will always be mean to her because they want what they can't have. It's not her fault. It's not even about her. It's about me. I wish she'd realize that.

I finally fall asleep while watching her angelic face while she sleeps.

In the morning, Keanna insists on bringing her flowers to Vegas so she has something pretty in the hotel room. We put them on the floor in the back seat of my truck, surrounded by our suitcases and bags to hold the vase upright. She doesn't say much as we get coffee and breakfast at a drive thru fast food place, but she keeps looking back at the flowers and smiling. I'm glad she seems a little better today.

After a couple hours of driving, I look over at her and grin. "Want to get fake IDs and go gambling once we get to Vegas?"

She rolls her eyes. "Breaking the law is against your Team Loco contract."

I sigh. "Yeah. And plus I'd have no idea where to get a fake ID."

She smiles a little, and it warms me up inside. "How are you doing?" I ask, trying to keep my voice level. I don't want to act like she's fragile and breakable because she's stronger than that. But I also would hate to say anything to make her feel worse. I know it's going to take her some time to get over what happened. I've seen her check Twitter a few times since we started driving.

She shrugs. "I'm fine."

"You don't really seem fine…" I say carefully.

She looks over at me and then unbuckles her seatbelt and slides across the front seat. She rests her head on my shoulder and loops her arm through mine. I love being close to her. I kiss her hair while keeping my eyes on the road.

"It just sucks," she says after a moment. "It just really sucks."

I'm not going to insult her by making up some stupid comment like *it'll get better,* when we both know these things take time to heal. "Yeah," I say. "It does."

Within minutes, she's asleep in the middle seat

of my truck, her hair falling over my shoulder. She's not stressed when she's sleeping, so I stay quiet and let her rest for the remainder of the journey.

"Baby," I whisper a few hours later. "We're here."

She sits up and blinks. "We're here already?"

"You slept a while," I say with a laugh.

She yawns. This is the moment I've been waiting for, seeing her face as we pull up to the famous city she's been wanting to visit. The barren Nevada landscape is a beautiful as it is different from Texas. We turn onto the Strip, which is really close to our hotel.

"Here we are," I say, watching her while I drive.

She gazes around, but her expression doesn't change. "Cool," she says after a while. "The mountains are pretty."

That's not even close to the type of response I thought she'd give me. I wanted to see her face light up. I wanted her to smile so big it reaches her eyes. I wanted her to do that cute bounce up and down in the seat thing she does when she's really excited. But even the allure of Vegas doesn't help take away her pain.

I grit my teeth as I follow the GPS to our hotel.

I wish I could personally curse out every asshole online who said those things to my girlfriend. I wish I could expose their secrets and embarrass them just as badly as they embarrassed her. I haven't even checked Twitter lately. I know it'll just piss me off more.

Still, I put on a smile and try to make Keanna's day better any way I can. Once again, we check into a new hotel, and she's happy when we're up on the nineteenth floor and she can look out at the city below.

I set her flowers on her nightstand and walk up behind her while she's gazing out the balcony window. I slide my hands around her and hold her tightly.

"I love you so much," I whisper.

"I love you, too."

I lean forward and kiss her cheek. "Is there anything I can do to make you feel better?"

She turns around to face me, and I keep my arms around her. Her hands wrap around my neck and she peers up at me with this sad smile.

"I'm okay. I'll be okay. I'm actually more worried about you."

I frown. "Why would you worry about me?"

She shrugs and looks away. "I don't know."

"Baby, I'm fine," I say, squeezing her closer to me. "I'll win this race. I'm not the least bit concerned."

She nods. "That's good."

Damn. Something tells me she didn't mean she was worried about my racing ability.

We settle into the hotel's oddly comfortable couch and watch some TV. The Vegas arena doesn't open up early and won't let us in to scope out the track like the other two had done, so there's nothing to do but hang with my girl. I'm totally fine with that, because she's the only thing in my life I truly care about.

Clay texts me around dinner time, asking if we want to go out to eat with them.

**Me:** No thanks, man. I'm spending time with my girl.

**Clay:** She feeling better?

**Me:** Honestly, not really. I thought Vegas would be special but it didn't help.

**Clay:** So make it special

**Clay:** Fuck the haters and make it special, dude.

I read his text and think it over in my mind.

**Me:** You're right. Thanks.

CHAPTER NINE

Keanna

Vegas is as beautiful as it looks in the movies. The only thing I didn't expect is that it seems a little smaller when you're walking down the infamous Vegas Strip. But the lights are shiny and colorful and fill you up with just enough whimsy to forget your problems. We'd tried visiting the cupcake place I want to try, but it was closed for a private party. I hope we'll get to go back to it before the trip is over.

Last night, Jett and I had gone with the guys to

get dinner at some restaurant that had acrobats performing all around us. After the last two miserable days I've had, I welcomed the distraction. I was able to put on a smile and actually mean half of it. It's kind of like magic, how getting out and doing something exciting makes you slip into a world of happiness that exists separately from your bleak real life. But as soon as we got back to the hotel last night, it all came back to me. Tidal waves of sadness pouring over me in ways I couldn't hold back. But I tried to. For Jett, I tried.

We'd stayed up late watching a movie in the hotel, cuddling in the bed surrounded by its many fluffy pillows. I loved the way his chest felt—strong and warm as I laid against him, but I still hurt.

He didn't ask me if everything was okay, or if I was feeling fine, or anything, so I think I did a good job of hiding this feeling that's grown so big inside of me that I fear it'll explode any day now.

Today is Friday, and Jett's Vegas race is tomorrow. We're supposed to do some sightseeing and find all the fun things you can do here when you're not old enough to drink, but we made a plan to sleep in late first. After all these days of waking up early to drive, it's nice to lay in bed with no schedule looming over you.

Only, I can't sleep in late.

I'm laying here in this comfortable hotel bed, next to Jett, who is perfect in every way, and yet I'm not sleeping. I'm staring at the ceiling and chewing on the inside of my lip. It's been hours since I last checked the drama online. I could tell Jett was watching me all night last night, hoping I wouldn't look at social media, so I didn't. But I can't hold back anymore. It's too tempting. It's so stupid, I know, but it is what it is.

I look over at Jett and he's sleeping peacefully, his breathing slow and steady. Carefully and slowly, I turn toward my nightstand and then wait, to make sure he's still asleep.

I reach for my phone, then open up Twitter. I used to check this thing all the time and never think twice about it. I used to scroll through tweets while waiting in line at the grocery store, or during commercial breaks on my favorite TV show. It's never mattered much until now.

Now, my hands are shaking and my stomach hurts and my heart pounds so hard I am certain it's going to wake up Jett. I close my eyes and take a deep breath, but it doesn't help. I have to see what these girls are saying about me online.

*I just got another update from the slut's old school-mates. She used to wear the same three outfits all the time and they were never washed.*

That one is kind of true. Many years of my life I only had one or two good pairs of jeans, and we only went to the laundromat whenever Mom had some quarters. For a while in ninth grade, I knew this girl who would let me spend the night and wash my clothes at her house. We were never really close friends though, I think she just felt sorry for me.

*She would sleep with any guy who asked. Figures.*

Not true. So not true. Ugh. I keep scrolling.

*Oh, and now I'm being told that she once gave a BJ to her high school teacher so he'd give her a passing grade in science. Why is Jett with this hoe? Like seriously???*

Also not true.

Even though I know my heart will break as I read through this crap, I can't help it. I can't stop myself. I have to see what they're saying about me. I have to know what everyone will be thinking if they see me at the races with Jett. What if Jett's manager gets word of this? What if Team Loco fires him because of his girlfriend's bad reputation?

The panic gets worse. Jett had to sign a contract with Team Loco saying he'd abide by laws and not make an embarrassment of the team with his actions. Surely that applies to the people he hangs out with too? His manager likes me, but probably not enough to overlook what everyone is saying.

I sit up in bed and throw off the covers, my skin suddenly so hot it's burning. Jett stays asleep as I pace the room, my phone gripped tightly in my hand. I can't do this to Jett. I'm going to ruin his career. It doesn't matter that most of the bad stuff is false, because some of it is true. I am not a nice normal girl with a normal family who deserves Jett and his wholesome image.

The lump in my throat threatens to cut off my airway and I put my hands on the glass of the balcony door, willing myself to take a deep breath. Nothing helps my heart slow down. Nothing makes my hands stop shaking.

I look back at Jett, and I'm glad he's asleep. He doesn't need to see me lose my freaking mind right now.

When my vision gets blurry from all the pacing and hyperventilating, I drop into a chair and look out the window, trying to focus on something outside that will take away this panic. A few moments later, I'm looking at my phone again. I hate myself. I hate how this addiction is too strong to break.

*Seriously, we need to start a petition to make Jett break up with her. He is so much better than her and he deserves better.*

That one is true.

Jett is better than this. He does deserve better. He deserves more. I look back at my boyfriend and tears fall down my cheek. I can't do it now because it would put a damper on his race tomorrow. I'm not sure how I'll survive doing what I know I have to do. We are neighbors. Our parents are best friends. Breaking up with Jett is going to be the hardest thing I've ever done.

I swallow and grit my teeth to keep my jaw from quivering. I swipe off the tears that are splashing on my shirt.

I guess I've known what I had to do all along. I don't deserve Jett. I don't deserve my family, either. Even though they adopted me, I'm a legal adult now so that's meaningless. Park and Becca just felt sorry for me—that's why they did it.

And Jett—he didn't know about my true past.

He didn't mean to get caught up with someone like me. Those girls on Twitter are mean, but they're right.

As soon as we get home, I'll have to break up with the guy I love more than anything. And then I'll have to leave, and let the people I care about go back to a life that's better off without me.

CHAPTER TEN

Jett

"You seem nervous."

I look over at Keanna, who's watching me with a frown. "Like… really nervous," she says. "You'll totally bounce back from that last race. I don't think you should be so worried about it."

Right. Tomorrow's race. That's what she thinks I'm nervous about. I take a deep breath and try to let some tension in my shoulders fall away. Now that she mentions it, I am nervous. My foot is twitching and my hands are tapping the steering wheel and there's not even any music playing on the radio. I probably shouldn't be driving right now with now nervous I am.

There's something in my pocket that Keanna doesn't know about. If she did, she'd probably know why I'm so nervous.

We've spent all day exploring Vegas and stopping at famous stores that have their own reality TV shows. We've eaten the famous cheese fries from that food show we like, and we took a trip through the famous pawn shop on the outskirts of town. The cupcake place was closed, but all in all, we've had a great day of being tourists. I haven't even thought of the race tomorrow because I'm not worried about it. I've raced hundreds of times in my life.

But tonight's event—I've never done it at all.

I know Keanna's hiding some of her pain through a fake smile, but I think she's feeling better. I did my best to make the day fun and eventful, and I've been careful not to mention anything that would make her think of Twitter. We will get through this tough time together and it'll blow over eventually. I think it'll really blow over after tonight.

Things are going to be perfect tonight.

The sun is starting to set, casting a beautiful glow on the city as I drive us back to the hotel. I'm running through the list of things in my head, hoping that the hotel's staff was able to set it all up like I'd asked them to. It was difficult planning something this big in secret, and I did most of it through text and when Keanna took a shower this morning. I want everything to be special for her. I hope I did this right.

I grab her hand as we walk in through the hotel's large lobby doors.

"We should go to bed early tonight," she says. "That way you can be fully rested for tomorrow."

"Mmhmm," I say. "Sounds like a good idea."

Little does she know, we probably won't sleep at all.

My pulse races as we step off the elevator and head toward our hotel room. I'm about to find out if my plan has been put into place by all the people I recruited to help me.

I drop the key card when I go to open the door, and Keanna bends down to pick it up for me. "You okay?" she asks.

"Perfect," I say. I slide the key into the lock and wait for the green light. I look at her as I push open the door. She smiles up at me. I draw in a deep breath. It's show time.

The hotel room smells like roses and vanilla, which is better than I'd imagined it would be. Every piece of furniture is decorated with dozens of scented candles, all lit and casting a romantic glow in the room. The bed has been sprinkled with rose petals, and a beautiful red rose bouquet sits on the table next to her other flowers. Soft music plays from a radio in the corner, and I grin when I see the centerpiece on our small dining table. A dozen Vegas cupcakes, bought in advance by me, and arranged in the shape of a heart.

Keanna gasps, her hands going to her mouth. Then she turns around. "What is this? It's not my birthday."

I can't hold back my grin even though my heart is pounding a mile a minute. I reach into my pocket and pull out the little velvet box that's been patiently waiting all week. I drop down on one knee, so unbelievably nervous, and open the box.

Keanna almost looks scared at first, and then tears fill her eyes, and then she covers her mouth and I can't read her expression.

"Keanna," I say, swallowing quickly to get my voice back. I'm so nervous I can barely function.

"You are the best part of me. I love you with all my heart and I want to be your husband for the rest of my life. Will you marry me?"

The next few seconds seem to slow to a crawl. Tears fall down her cheeks, and I think they're happy tears, but I'm not so sure. I'm so nervous that she might say no, and all I want is to hear the yes. My hand shakes as I hold up the ring I picked out months ago. Finally, her hands fall from her face. This is it. Now she'll say yes.

"I was going to break up with you," she says.

My whole world seems to crack in half. "What?" I say, still on my knee, my heart rocketing around in my chest. This can't be happening.

She shrugs and another tear rolls down her beautiful face. "I thought you deserved better than me," she says, looking at the floor. "I thought it would be best to break up with you when we get home, and now you just proposed and I don't even know what to say."

"Oh my God," I stammer. "Why..? I—"

She chokes back a sob. "I want to marry you more than anything, Jett," she says as she wipes away tears. "I just feel like you can do better. I know you can do better."

"I don't want anyone else," I say, the words

tumbling out of the deepest parts of my soul. "I only want you. And anyone who thinks differently can piss off. You are my angel and my soul mate and I just want you."

A soft smile breaks through her tears. "Are you sure?"

I hold up the ring higher as if this shiny huge diamond is all the proof I need. "Yes."

She smiles. "Are we doing this?"

I grin back at her. "Well, you haven't said yes yet."

She drops to her knees in front of me and throws her arms around my neck. "Yes," she whispers. That single word wraps up all the pieces of my newly shattered heart and binds them back together. I hold onto her tightly and tell her how much I love her. When she pulls back, I take her hand and put the ring on her finger.

"Thank you," I say. "For the most terrifying few seconds of my life."

She chuckles, her gaze focused on her new engagement ring. She looks just as I pictured she would look when I bought it. "I can't believe you want to marry me," she says softly. "After all the drama…"

"That was nothing," I say. "You and me, we're

perfect. We don't have drama. Let others create whatever they want to make their lives more miserable, but when we're together, we're happy. And we're all that matters, babe."

I dry her tears with my thumb and pull her closer, placing my lips on hers. "For better or worse, I want you Keanna. Especially in the worse times. When everything else goes wrong, you are the only person I can count on."

She climbs into my lap and now we're both on the floor, clinging to each other like we can't possibly stand to let go. It's the best place in the world to be.

"Jett," she says, peering at me with those eyes that melt my heart.

"Yes, love?"

"Will you take my phone and delete the Twitter app?"

I laugh. "Sure. I'll delete mine, too."

"Perfect." She wraps her arms around my neck and pulls me up against her. "For better or worse," she says.

I kiss her hair. "And forever and ever."

## Don't miss Jett and Keanna's final book: Forever and a Day

The whole motocross world is watching us. Half of Jett's fans are happy for him. The other half are mad at me, the girl he just proposed to. They don't think I'm good enough to marry the fastest racer in Texas. Or they think it should be them with the Tiffany engagement ring instead of me. But Jett disagrees.

Maybe we're too young. Maybe we don't know what we're doing.

But this is our life and we're going to live it the way we want to.

Until death do us part.

KEEP READING FOR A PREVIEW OF
FOREVER AND A DAY

Keanna

My teeth bite down on my lip as I hold the nail up against the drywall. No matter how many times I've done this, I'm always afraid I'll smash my thumb with the hammer. Coordination isn't exactly a talent of mine, which is why I don't ride dirt bikes like the rest of my family. After a few timid taps, the nail is secure and I remove my fingers and then drive the nail further into the wall. I reach for the framed document and line it up, making sure it's perfectly straight. This wall decoration is more important than a piece of art. It's an accomplishment.

Stepping back, I can't help but crack a smile as I admire it. This feels exactly as cool as Bree said it would. My name is on an official diploma.

Sure, it's just an associate's degree, but it's better than nothing. I'll get my bachelors in a couple of years and I'll hang that on the wall, too. After all, that's what an office is for, right?

I'm so psyched that I recently got my own office at The Track. While the facility has a very uninspired name—I mean seriously, who names a dirt bike track *The Track*—it's my favorite place in the world. It's where I plan to work until my parents retire and then the place will be handed down to my boyfriend and me.

The Track is the motocross facility that was founded by my dad and my boyfriend's dad, who are both former professional motocross racers. I guess Jett is my fiancé, but it still feels weird calling him that, and I find myself calling him *boyfriend* instead of *fiancé*. He proposed a while back with the most gorgeous ring ever, but then we never talked about it much. Life has been too busy. I've been in college classes and he's been traveling the country racing dirt bikes for Team Loco. I'm actually at The Track far more than Jett is, and he grew up here.

We're a top-notch facility that has four different motocross tracks, a gym that's open to the public, a daycare for when parents are riding or racing, and a little shop up front that sells motocross gear. The world of motocross was totally new to me when I moved here to Lawson, Texas, but now it's my life. Sometimes it feels like a little *too* much of my life, but I'm grateful for it nonetheless.

My office used to be a storage closet, but after my dad and Jace agreed to promote me to assistant manager of the entire facility, they also decided that I needed a real office. The construction only took a few days, and now I have my own place with my own diploma, and an actual salary that goes with it. No more working hourly for me.

I've only been in here for a few months, and my office still isn't perfectly set up the way I'd like it to be. That's the thing about Pinterest inspiration photos. They look so beautiful and cozy but when you try to implement the same exact design, it looks off. Like a little girl wearing her mom's high heels. It doesn't fit right because you have no idea what you're doing.

But at least it's mine. These last few years of living here with my adoptive parents have been the most amazing years of my life. I finally feel secure. Safe. Having grown up with Dawn, my biological mother who was so incompetent at raising me that we often lived in our car or some random man's house, it feels good to finally be settled. My new parents, Becca and Park, have done everything possible to make sure I feel like a part of the family. And I do. Most days I don't even think about Dawn anymore. It's been a couple of years since I last heard from her, when she called me up on New Years to ask for some money after abandoning me with Becca and Park. Yep. She abandoned me. She met Becca, who invited us over to lunch, and then my mom just left, leaving me to fend for myself. It wasn't long after that I was adopted by the very couple who took me in after Dawn abandoned me.

That was my old life.

Good freaking riddance.

This is my new life.

With classes over, the summer break is starting and I'll get a little time off from college. I try to travel with Jett to some of his races, but I'm also needed here at my job. It's a complicated balance, but I do what I can.

Jett is a sponsored motocross racer for Team Loco, which means they travel around and race the supercross and motocross circuits every year. Each season is around 25 races long, and at the end of it, whoever has the most points wins the overall series. Jett and the other members of Team Loco have collectively earned way more points than the other racers, as per usual. Jett is amazing. He's kind and warm and thoughtful, and he's a badass racer too.

I love him so much and can't wait to marry him. But for now, we're just taking things slow, I guess. He has racing, and I have work and school. There's plenty of time to settle down and live the married life later on. I'm only twenty-one, after all. I don't have to get married right away. But sometimes it is weird knowing that we're engaged and we're not even planning a wedding.

Jett didn't have to give me a ring to make me want to stay in a relationship with him. He pulled me out of a dark time in my life and made me see that life could be happy, fun, and beautiful. I would stay with him no matter what—rich or poor, ring or not. He is one hundred percent my soul mate.

My office phone rings, pulling me out of my thoughts about Jett. I lean over and answer it, seeing on the caller ID that it's only the front desk calling me and not a customer.

"What's up?" I say.

"Have you been online lately?" Morgan says in this weirdly high-pitched voice that sets my senses on high alert. She's the girl my mom hired to replace me when I moved from working the front desk to being a manager. We're only about a thirty second walk away from each other, but she can't leave her spot at the front desk to come talk to me in case a customer walks in, so she calls me.

"No," I say, sitting in my desk chair. "Is it something about The Track?"

She pauses for a split second and that's all it takes to make my stomach tighten. We live in a glass bubble. Sure, it's just a glass bubble that only the world of motocross pays attention to, and it's not like we're worldwide celebrities or anything, but it's enough to make you stressed out. My boyfriend is famous in his line of work, and his dad, Jace Adams, was also famous back when he was younger. They've graced the cover of motocross magazines, DVDs, posters, and t-shirts. The sport of motocross worships Team Loco.

By association, The Track is also pretty popular since it was founded by two former professional motocross racers. My dad was also famous back in his day, and he's Jace's best friend. While most of the attention we get is from the fans, there's always jealous, hateful people and internet trolls who try to take us down. Especially me, a motocross girlfriend.

So when Morgan pauses just for a second, a familiar dread builds up in my chest. I know it's about me. It has to be. "It's not about the track," she says.

I let out a long breath and slink further down my chair. The screensaver on my computer is showing a slideshow of photos, most of them featuring Jett and me. A few show my little brother, or pictures of our past vacations. All I have to do is pull up the internet and search my name and find out what's going on. But *ugh*, I don't want to.

"How bad is it?" I ask.

"Not too bad," she says, but I don't believe her. "Just some stupid article."

"Where?"

"Motocross Girls."

"Thanks," I say, hanging up the phone.

Motocross Girls is supposed to be all about empowering women in the sport of motocross and lifting each other up. At least that's what their website claims to be about. In reality, they love to post articles tearing down the girlfriends of motocross racers. Because I guess they only care about women when they're talking about themselves. Not anyone else.

I've had this talk with every girlfriend on Team Loco. As soon as one of Jett's teammates starts dating someone, I've felt it is my duty to warn them about how toxic and heartbreaking it can be to be a motocross girlfriend. It shouldn't be like this, but it is. The fans get jealous. They hate you because you're dating their celebrity crush. They turn you into some monster in their heads and then try to find any way possible to insult you online.

I wish I could ignore this news, but I know I need to look it up. I have to know what people are saying about me, what the customers who walk into the building will be thinking when they see me.

I pull up the website and the first thing I see is the title of their newest blog post.

. . .

*Keanna Park – Legitimate Fiancé or Hired Pawn?*

I roll my eyes at the absurdity of that title. Then I read.

*It's no secret that talented hottie Jett Adams has been off the market for a while now. After earning a reputation as a player, the bad boy racer settled down with a mysterious new girl that no one had heard of before. Millions of hearts were broken, but we thought she'd go away sooner or later. The southern girl from a broken home doesn't have much to offer Jett, after all.*

*But then they got engaged, and those broken hearts shattered to pieces. Was this it? Was Jett Adams actually going to tie the knot with some backwoods girl who doesn't deserve him?*

*Ladies, I think the answer is no.*

*I don't know the reason – maybe focusing on his career? – but Jett clearly just wanted to take himself off the market, or at least make it look like it. So he found a girl to be his "girlfriend." Now she's his "fiancé," and it's been over a year since the massive Tiffany diamond ring appeared on Keanna's finger, but guess what? No wedding has been planned. Sources close to the couple (if* you can call them that) have confirmed that no Save the Dates have been sent out, no wedding planning has taken place, and there's absolutely no talk of them actually tying the knot.

We've all been bamboozled.

That's good news, girls. Jett only wants us to think he's off the market. Clearly he's not.

I wonder how much Keanna got paid to go along with this ruse? It's a story like something straight out of a pathetic Hallmark movie. Only in the real world, Keanna, he's not going to fall in love with you. You are just a business transaction.

Case closed.

Jett

I wake up to my phone buzzing on the nightstand. It's in danger of sliding right off the thing, which means it's been buzzing for a while now. My first thought is that something must be wrong with Keanna, but she'd just come over here if that were the case. Now that I'm home and not on the road, we live next door to each other.

Well, there's a massive motocross track between our houses, but still. She doesn't need to call me, she can just show up. It's not uncommon for me to wake up in the morning and see her downstairs having coffee with my mom. So the source of the dozens of text messages must be from someone else.

I yawn and sit up and stretch out my aching muscles. I definitely went too hard at the gym last night. It's been three weeks since the spring racing series ended and I was so happy to finally be back home that I let my workout routine slip a bit. Last night I tried to make up for three weeks of no workouts and I'm paying for it today.

I blink away my exhaustion and look at the phone.

The phone buzzing didn't come from one person texting me repeatedly, but rather seven people texting me all at once.

It's too early for this crap.

I set the phone back down. I'll brush my teeth and take a hot shower, and then I'll read whatever drama is going on. With motocross, it's always something.

One of the other motocross racers might have gotten a DUI, or broken a bone or something. News travels fast in this sport, and everyone always wants to gossip about it. I know I'm speaking for all four members of Team Loco when

I say I wish we could just keep the sport about racing and not all the stupid personal drama that goes with it. Whatever has happened this time is probably just as stupid and pointless as the last few times that something went viral and everyone freaked out.

I dry my hair off with a towel and put on some shorts and a shirt. I feel bad because it's almost eleven in the morning and I've slept pretty late. I don't technically work at my parent's business because my job is motocross racing, but I know my girlfriend gets there at nine in the morning and I like to hang out with her when I can.

I haven't spent nearly enough time with her this year. Getting sponsored to race for Team Loco has been a dream, and racing professionally is literally what I was born to do. But it takes away precious time with my girl, and I need to make sure I make our relationship a priority. My dad taught me that a long time ago. I can't just assume she'll always be there waiting on me. She deserves someone who makes time for her. So I feel more than guilty that I slept in late today. No more late-night workout sessions at the gym. From now until the summer racing series starts in two weeks, I'm going to spend every waking second with my girl.

On the walk over to The Track, I unlock my phone and check out the stupid texts. What I read makes me stop short. All of my friends are telling me about a new article posted on some girly motocross website.

I click on the link and skim the article, which makes the hairs on my neck stand on end.

Whoever wrote this was trashing Keanna. My girlfriend – my fiancé – the greatest person I've ever met in my life. They're straight trashing her and questioning our relationship.

White hot rage fills my veins. I grip my phone tightly and try not to fling it across the field in front of me. That wouldn't solve anything, but it'd sure feel good for about half a second. Instead, I shove it in my pocket and walk faster. The Track's main building is just a few yards away and maybe I can get to Keanna before she finds out about this article.

Who am I kidding? She'll know by now.

Why, oh why did I sleep in late? I should have been up early, bringing her coffee to work. I could have prevented this. Well, I could have tried to. News like this doesn't stay a secret very long, and I'm sure she'd have seen it sooner or later.

Morgan gives me a weird smile when I walk

into the building. "Hey, Jett," she says, waving one hand.

Damn. She knows. Her normal cheery demeanor is gone, wiped away with the knowledge of the latest social media attack on my life.

"Good morning," I say, choosing to pretend that everything is fine.

I walk down the hall that's lined with black and white floor tiles, the walls decorated with framed photos of my dad, Park, and me at various races. Keanna's office door is mostly closed, only cracked open a few inches. My knuckles rap on the door.

"Babe?"

"I'm in here," she says.

I push open the door and smile at her. Keanna's wearing a bright blue T-shirt with The Track's logo on the front. Her brown hair is pulled into a messy scrunch on top of her head. She's sitting at her desk, her feet propped up on the filing cabinet. Her shoes are kicked off on the floor, revealing her pink and black polka dot socks. She looks at me over the top of her coffee mug.

"What's up," she says dryly.

"You've seen it," I say, walking into the small room.

She shrugs.

I lean over and kiss the top of her head. She smells like coffee and apple shampoo. "Don't let it bother you, baby."

She shrugs again. "I'm not bothered."

"You look bothered."

She rolls her eyes.

I sit on her desk, wishing she'd look at me, but instead she's just focusing on a pen, spinning it around and around on top of her desk.

"You know they're just trying to start shit," I say softly. "Their opinions are just that – opinions. They're wrong about all of it, and you will be my wife and you're the only person I care about. Not them, not their fake drama."

She looks up at me now, her dark chestnut eyes filled with an emotion I can't quite understand. I know I'll never fully get what she's gone through and how she feels. She had a hard childhood, and mine was privileged. She's been through hell, and I haven't. She's the strongest person I've ever met.

"I know who you are," she says slowly. "And I know who I am. I know what we feel for each other. I know the facts." Her shoulders fall as she stares at the pen between her fingers. She spins it and watches it blur in a circle. "I just hate that this other part of our lives—this part that isn't real—is thrown into the spotlight so often. Why do these people care about us? Why is it news?"

She shakes her head. "Why can't they just leave us alone?"

I lean forward and take her chin in my hand, tilting her face up to look at me. "Baby, I'm sorry."

Tears well up in her eyes and she blinks them away. Then, one second later, she sits up straight and dons a smile. It's like she's just decided to shove all bad thoughts out of her mind.

"It's not your fault," she says sweetly as she leans up and kisses me. "I'm hungry. Let's get some lunch."

But that's where she's wrong. It is my fault. I'm the professional racer here. I'm the reason the media cares about her. It's all my fault and I need to make it right.

Keanna and I walk out to my truck and drive into town to get some lunch. The whole time, I'm thinking about what I can do to put an end to the speculation and drama about how we're not married yet. I am more than ready to marry this girl. I meant it when I proposed, and then life got in the way. Not anymore. It's time to plan this wedding.

It's time to make this relationship unbreakable.

FOREVER AND A DAY CHAPTER 3

Keanna

It's rare to get a Friday night off work. Usually there's a race scheduled for the weekend, and that means it's all hands on deck as we get the place ready for an influx of thousands of racers and spectators. But the local racing season has just come to a close, much like the professional racing season, and this is one of those rare weekends where I'll get to lounge around and do nothing.

To add icing to the top of this good-luck-sundae, Jett is also home for the weekend. We'll have two full days of no work, no racing, no motocross. Just Jett and me.

I don't realize how excited I am about this until Jett tells me that he's taking me to dinner tonight. A little thrill of excitement runs through me when I read his text. We haven't had a real date in a long time. I mean, sure, we go out to eat all the time when we're traveling, and I see him every day when he's home. When I visit him on the road, we'll go sight-seeing and enjoy being tourists, which is kind of date-like. But it's not as good as a date in our hometown.

Because when we're out somewhere else, traveling for Jett's work, it's all about the motocross. We're on a tight schedule that revolves around his racing, traveling, and PR projects for Team Loco. No matter where we go, we're always swamped with fans who want to take Jett's attention away from me. Date nights on the road aren't as fun.

Date nights at home, here in the tiny town of Lawson, Texas, are what I look forward to. Sure, Jett's still famous here in town, but everyone already knows him. These people have seen him grow up from when he was a baby, so he's not such big news anymore. We can be ourselves here in town.

Before I can get ready for my date, I help my mom in the kitchen by washing the dishes and cleaning up a bit. Becca is my adoptive mom, but I've gotten used to calling her Mom instead of Becca. It's what she wants to be called. The same thing with Park, who I now call Dad. I've never had a dad in my life, so that one was a little easier to get used to—but sometimes, even two years later, I'll call Becca *Mom*, and I'll have a quick flashback of my biological mother, Dawn. It always makes me cringe. I wish I wasn't adopted. I wish I was Becca and Park's real-life-DNA-related daughter. Things would be easier that way.

Mom's trying to get my baby brother Elijah to eat his veggies by singing and dancing and pretending it's a fun experience. She's not very successful. At one point, Elijah's chubby fist shoves some broccoli into his mouth and my mom claps. Then he spits it out and laughs.

I am definitely okay with waiting a while to have kids. They are so much work it's ridiculous. I can barely remember to keep myself fed each day, much less worry about another kid. My adoptive parents had tried forever to conceive their own child, but it just wasn't in the cards. A year ago, Jett's mom gave Becca the generous gift of being a surrogate, and then Elijah was born.

"Thanks for doing that, honey," Mom tells me

as I'm putting up the clean dishes from the dishwasher.

"Need anything else done?" I ask. Even though I'm technically a part of the family ever since she and Park legally adopted me, I still feel this compulsive need to make sure I'm proving myself worthy of living here. I keep things clean, I do the grocery shopping, and I help out in any way I can.

Mom heaves a sigh and tucks some hair behind her ear. She looks older, somehow. Older than she normally does. I stare at her a moment trying to figure out what's different. Her hair is the same light brown as always, streaked with a little bit of gray, and she doesn't seem to have a lot of wrinkles or anything. She just looks off. I guess she's exhausted from Elijah.

"You okay?" I ask her.

She gives me a smile that seems a little forced. "Yep, I'm good. You doing something fun tonight?"

"Jett and I are going out to dinner," I say, bending to pick up some broccoli my brother just tossed on the floor. "But I can stay here and help if you need."

"No, no," Mom says, waving her hand at me. "You need a night out. Go have fun."

She would tell me if she needed help. I try not

to feel guilty as I head back to my bedroom and choose an outfit for tonight. I'm not sure where we're going, but there's not many places in Lawson. I don't need to dress nice like I would if we were in LA or something. I put on a black skirt and a dark blue tank top, then slip into some sandals. The great thing about Texas is that it's always warm even in the spring time.

Even though we live next to each other, Jett always insists on coming to my house and picking me up on nights that we've declared official date nights. He doesn't like it if I walk over and meet him halfway, even though when it's not an official date night, that's what we do all the time.

I stand at my front door and wait for him to get here, expecting to see his truck pull into the driveway. Instead, he comes over on a four-wheeler.

I step outside and cock my head. "What's this?" I call out, but Jett can't hear me over the engine.

He cuts the motor, climbs off the shiny blue ATV, and jogs up to my front porch. He's looking sexy as always and I know for a fact it didn't take him longer than thirty seconds to get ready. He's wearing a black T-shirt and jeans. His dirty blonde hair is hanging wildly around his face like it doesn't have to obey the rules. He doesn't have to try at all, and yet he's the cutest guy I've ever seen.

"Hey, babe," he says, kissing me quickly on the lips. "Ready?"

"Please tell me we're not taking a four-wheeler into town?" I say, tossing a look at what's parked in my driveway.

Jett grins. "Who said we're going into town?"

I put a hand on my hip. "I thought it was official date night?"

Jett's grin slides into a coy smirk and he wiggles his eyebrows. "It is official date night. Let's go."

Reluctantly, I crawl on the back of the ATV and wrap my arms around Jett's stomach. He drives us straight toward The Track, and I'm more confused than ever when he turns and heads toward the biggest motocross track on the facility. He rides slowly over the finish line jump and then takes us further and further down the track until we're at the back of the property. There's a large wooden fence here that separates our land from the fields behind it where cows graze. But before you get to the fence, there's some scattered oak trees that line the perimeter of the track. I've never really been back here before.

Jett turns to the left and drives a little further,

and then I see what's going on here. My heart floods with love for this guy. Jett rolls us to a stop. In front of me is a little clearing, a circle of grass that's lined with ancient and gorgeous old trees that were spared when the land was cleared for the track.

In the middle of the circle is a large plaid blanket, a picnic basket, pillows, and more that I can't take in all at once because my eyes are watering with unshed tears. Jett climbs off the four-wheeler and reaches out a hand to me.

"I wanted official date night to be better than dinner at some boring restaurant in town," he says.

I take his hand and he helps me off the monstrosity of an ATV. "I wanted tonight to be special."

I blink away my tears and reach up and kiss him, feeling an overwhelming surge of emotions that take over my heart. Sometimes I get upset, and even a little resentful that I can't spend as much alone time with my boyfriend like other people do in normal non-famous relationships. But it's times like these that I realize I have the best relationship there is.

Jett's picnic dinner consists of takeout food from my favorite Chinese place and cupcakes from my favorite bakery. The four corners of the soft blanket are held down with fake candles that flicker in the night as if they were real flames.

"I didn't want to risk burning the place down," Jett says when I pick up a plastic candle and look at it.

I laugh. "Smart thinking."

He sets his phone to a music playlist that fills the air with soft music, and then we sit on the blanket. I reach for my food, but Jett doesn't get his right away. He's staring at me in this weird way that makes heat rise to my cheeks.

"What?" I say. "Is there something on my face?"

He shakes his head. "I was supposed to wait until after dinner…"

I lift an eyebrow as fear trickles down my spine. "Wait for what? To do what?"

He bites his lip and glances down at his lap. I'm pretty sure he's not about to break up with me or anything, but why is he being so weird? "Jett?" I say, my voice sounding timid and scared.

He takes a deep breath and reaches into his pocket. He pulls out a teal jewelry box and looks up at me, a hint of something sexy in his eyes. I relax a little.

He leans closer to me. We're sitting right next

to each other on the blanket, and I can smell his cologne, see the flecks of gold in his eyes. He opens the box.

Inside is a beautiful sparkling ring, white gold and lined with little diamonds. I look up at him, a little confused. I mean, he's already proposed. So what is this?

"I want to start planning the wedding," he says, looking deep into my eyes. "I don't want to just be engaged anymore. I want to be married."

I bite the inside of my lip to stop my smile from getting embarrassingly huge. "I didn't realize how much I wanted to hear that until now," I say softly.

Jett brushes the hair from my face, tucking it behind my ear. His fingers are rough, calloused from years of dirt bike racing, but I still close my eyes at the feeling of his skin on mine. "I dropped out of the summer series."

I startle, my eyes jolting open. "What?"

Jett says the same thing again.

"Why?" This is so not good.

He just smiles and wets his lips. "I told my manager I needed some time off. For personal reasons." He leans over and kisses my cheek. "We have four months until I have to go back and race the fall series. Let's plan our wedding and get married before then."

I'm not sure if I want to cry, or laugh, or what. All I know is that I am ridiculously happy. I take the ring box and run my finger over the sparkling diamonds. This is the matching wedding band that goes to my engagement ring. At the end of the summer, I'll get to wear both of them.

"What do you think?" Jett asks.

I answer by throwing my arms around his shoulders and crushing my lips to his.

Amy Sparling is the bestselling author of books for teens and the teens at heart. She lives on the coast of Texas with her family, her spoiled rotten pets, and a huge pile of books. She graduated with a degree in English and has worked at a bookstore, coffee shop, and a fashion boutique. Her fashion skills aren't the best, but luckily she turned her love of coffee and books into a writing career that means she can work in her pajamas. Her favorite things are coffee, book boyfriends, and Netflix binges.

She's always loved reading books from R. L. Stine's Fear Street series, to The Baby Sitter's Club series by Ann, Martin, and of course, Twilight. She started writing her own books in 2010 and now publishes several books a year. Amy loves getting messages from her readers and responds to every single one! Connect with her on one of the links below.